Spirulina and the Pirates

Mermaid Rock

Be sure to read:

Spirulina and the Haunted Shipwreck

... and lots, lots more!

Spirulina and the Pirates

Kelly McKain
illustrated by Cecilia Johansson

■SCHOLASTIC

To Millie, love Kelly

Scholastic Children's Books,
Commonwealth House, 1-19 New Oxford Street,
London, WC1A 1NU, UK
a division of Scholastic Ltd
London ~ New York ~ Toronto ~ Sydney ~ Auckland
Mexico City ~ New Delhi ~ Hong Kong

First published by Scholastic Ltd, 2003

Text copyright © Kelly McKain, Prospero Promotions Limited, 2003
Illustrations copyright © Cecilia Johansson, 2003

ISBN 0 439 97855 6

Printed and bound by Oriental Press, Dubai, UAE

10 9 8 7 6 5 4 3 2 1

The rights of Kelly McKain and Cecilia Johansson to be identified as the author and
illustrator of this work respectively have been asserted by them in accordance with the
Copyright, Designs and Patents Act, 1988.

☆ Chapter One ☆

Spirulina wriggled around on Mermaid
Rock. Barnacles were digging into her
beautiful blue-green tail. "Being a mermaid
is so boring," she grumbled.

Coralie and Shelle, her two sisters, tried
to ignore her.

"Oh, Spirulina, do sit still," said Coralie bossily.

"But my tail's sore," Spirulina said grumpily. "It's stupid to sit on a jaggedy craggedy rock all day. We could be splashing about in the sea!"

"Yuck! Seawater messes up my hair," said Shelle, shocked.

"You two can sit there preening
yourselves and getting tail ache if you like,"
Spirulina told her sisters, "but I've got more
important things to do."

"Such as what?" asked Shelle.

"I'm going to be a pirate," said Spirulina.

Coralie and Shelle laughed daintily.
"You? A pirate?"

"Yes, me," huffed Spirulina. "I'm going to build a pirate ship and sail the seven seas!"

"But you're only a little mermaid," giggled Coralie. "You're not brave enough."

"I am! You'll see!" cried Spirulina, sticking her tongue out at them. And with that she flicked her tail and dived into the sparkling sea.

☆ ☆ ☆

All morning Spirulina collected pieces of
driftwood. Then she set about hammering
and sawing and nailing them together to
make a pirate
ship.

She found an old shirt
that had blown off
the beach and
used it as a sail.

"I name this ship the SS *Spirulina*," she cried in delight.

"That silly boat will sink in a moment," called Coralie from Mermaid Rock.

"That sail's too tattered to hold the wind," shouted Shelle. "You won't get anywhere."

Spirulina frowned.
What if Coralie and
Shelle were right?
What if the SS *Spirulina*
did sink? What if the
sail *was* too tattered?

Suddenly a strong wind blew up and the little boat began to skim away over the ocean. Spirulina laughed with delight.

"Anchors away!" she called, tying on her pirate headscarf. "I'm afloat, me shivering sisters! I'm a-sailing away to adventures on the high seas! I'll see you later!"

There was plenty to do on board the pirate ship. Spirulina tickled a trout...

...juggled some jellyfish...

...and danced
with dolphins.

She swashbuckled
with seals...

...and sang sea
shanties.

At lunchtime, she took out her seaweed sandwiches and shared  them with the seagulls.

Spirulina yawned. "It's hard work being a pirate," she said sleepily. "I think I'll curl up here on the deck for a snooze."

As the waves gently rocked her boat, Spirulina fell fast asleep. She didn't know it, but she was in terrible danger.

☆ Chapter Two ☆

Splish! Splash! Splosh!

Spirulina was woken by drops of rain falling on to her face.

She sat up with a start and stared around in horror. She had drifted far out to sea! She couldn't see Mermaid Rock any more. In fact, she couldn't see anywhere any more!

"Pirates don't panic," she told herself firmly. "I'll just set sail and hope that the shore comes into view."

But then disaster struck. Black storm clouds gathered above Spirulina's little boat. Crackle-crackle-SNAP! Lightning lit the stormy sky. Rumble-rumble-BOOM! Thunder rolled around her.

Then the rain lashed down. A fierce wind whipped Spirulina's hair and face. Wild waves battered her little boat. She clung to the mast as the SS *Spirulina* began to sink.

"Oh, what shall I do?" she cried. "Lost in thunder and lightning! Sinking in a storm!" Two fat tears rolled down her face. "Coralie and Shelle were right," she sniffled. "I'm not brave enough to be a pirate!"

With that, she began to sob and sob. In fact, she was crying so hard that she almost missed the blurry shape on the horizon. She wiped her eyes and squinted through the rain.

"A ship!" she cried. "Thank goodness! Over here! Over here!"

The ship came closer...

...and closer...

...until it was right beside Spirulina's boat.

"Pirates!" gasped Spirulina.

A bearded man leaned over the side of the mighty galleon.

"Ahoy there!" he bellowed. "What have we here? Shipmate Shifty, come and look at this!"

A pink-faced man appeared. "That's a little lost mermaid, Captain Curly," he said.

"We were just going your way, me little mer-mate," roared Captain Curly. "Climb aboard and bring your vessel. We'll take you home."

Spirulina wasn't sure whether she could trust the pirates … but she didn't have any choice. "Thank you," she called.

Captain Curly helped her aboard the pirate ship.

Chapter Three

"Pretty Polly!"

Spirulina whirled round. She saw a parrot in a cage swinging from the rigging.

"Pretty Polly!" the parrot squawked again.

"Shut up, Polly," snarled Captain Curly. "You're not a Pretty Polly, you're a scrawny old bird!"

Spirulina looked at the parrot. Its eyes were sad and its feathers were falling off.

"Pretty Polly!" it squawked again.

"That parrot's driving me mad," roared Captain Curly. "Bony Boson, throw it in the brig!"

"Aye, aye, Captain!" Bony Boson took the parrot cage and threw it into the brig.

"That's not a nice way to treat a parrot," cried Spirulina, but the pirates ignored her.

"Hey, little lost mermaid," bellowed Captain Curly, "show us some mermaiding."

"Aye, give us a tune, go on," called Bony Boson.

"Sit over there and comb your hair," ordered Shipmate Shifty.

"I'm not that sort of mermaid," said Spirulina crossly. "I sail the seven seas and have adventures and—"

"Ha, ha, ha!" roared the pirates. "Well, if you're not going to do what a mermaid should then we'll have to lock you up with that silly parrot!"

Then Bony Boson picked Spirulina up,
tossed her into the brig and turned the key.

"That's not a nice way to treat a
mermaid!" shouted Spirulina.

But the pirates just roared with laughter.
Captain Curly tapped his wooden leg on
the deck. "Come on, lads! Let's sleep here
until the storm has passed. Then we'll put
our wicked plan into action!"

Spirulina gulped. What wicked plan?

☆ ☆ ☆

"Those pirates are really terrible," sighed
Spirulina.

"I agree!" squawked the parrot.

Spirulina stared at it, amazed. "But,
Polly," she cried, "I thought you could only
say 'Pretty Polly'."

"That's all I ever say to *them*," said the
parrot smugly. "It really drives them crazy!
And besides, my name's not
Polly, it's Jennifer."

"Nice to meet you, Jennifer," said Spirulina. "I'm Spirulina."

"How do you do?" squawked Jennifer. "It's lovely to have  someone sensible to talk to at last. I hate being stuck in this horrible cage. That's why all my feathers are falling off."

"I can help you," said Spirulina. She pulled a pair of pliers from her tool belt and prised the bars of the cage apart.

Jennifer tottered out and stretched
her wings.

"Ah, that's better," she sighed happily.
"Thank you,
Spirulina."

Spirulina grinned. "Now all we have to do
is escape and find out what
those wicked pirates are
up to."

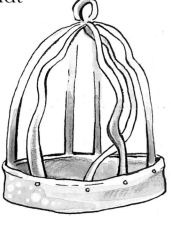

"I know what they're up to," squawked Jennifer. "They're sailing to Mermaid Rock, to steal the purses of those two preening mermaids."

Spirulina gasped in horror. "Those two preening mermaids are my sisters Coralie and Shelle!" she exclaimed. "Oh, Jennifer, we've got to stop the pirates!"

⭐ Chapter Four ⭐

As the rain drummed down on to the brig, Spirulina came up with a pirate-busting plan, which she whispered to Jennifer.

"That's brilliant!" squawked Jennifer. "But first we've got to get out of here! I think I could squeeze through those window bars and steal the keys."

They listened to check that the coast was clear.

Sure enough, the sound of snoozing pirates filled the air.

Jennifer breathed in, folded her wings and wriggled between two of the bars.

She flew across the deck
and took the bunch
of keys from
the ring at
Captain
Curly's waist.

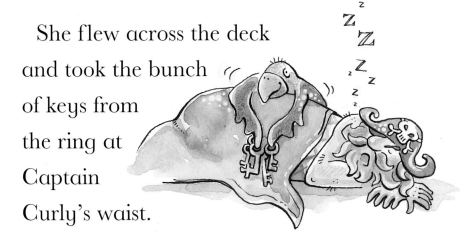

Then she zoomed
back and set
Spirulina free.

Spirulina crept out of the brig.

She sneaked round to the galley and found a huge vat of oil. Grinning, she poured the oil all along the deck and down the plank.

Next, she tipped the pirates' rum into the sea.

Then she filled up the flagon with seawater and a couple of baby crabs.

Meanwhile, Jennifer set a trap with her cage.

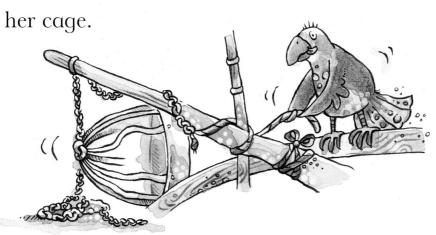

Last of all, Spirulina took out her hammer and quietly tapped a nail into the bottom of Captain Curly's peg leg.

They just made it
back into the brig
before the
pirates
woke up.

"Land ahoy, me hearties!" Captain
Curly bellowed. "The storm has passed
and Mermaid Rock is straight ahead!"

When Coralie and Shelle spotted the
pirate ship they started
to scream.

"Surrender your purses, my lovelies,"
roared Captain Curly, "or prepare to feel
my silver cutlass on your
pretty necks!"

"Yeah, hand 'em over," shouted Shipmate Shifty.

"Help! Help!" cried Coralie. "Wicked pirates are stealing our precious jewels!"

"Help! Help!" shrieked Shelle. "Someone save us!"

☆ Chapter Five ☆

Spirulina came dashing out of the brig. "Spirulina to the rescue!" she cried.

"And Jennifer to the rescue too," squawked the parrot, flapping along behind her.

"No mermaid gets the better of me!" roared Captain Curly. He lunged towards Spirulina, his silver cutlass flashing.

But he didn't get anywhere. The nail Spirulina had hammered into his peg leg pinned him to the deck! He was FURIOUS. "Get 'em lads!" he bellowed.

Shipmate Shifty and Bony Boson ran at Spirulina.

Bony Boson slid on the oily deck – and fell straight into Jennifer's trap.

Jennifer tugged a rope and the cage lifted off the ground.

"Ha! See how you like it," she squawked, winching Bony Boson up the rigging. He swung back and forth miserably, waving his skinny arms and legs.

Shipmate Shifty grabbed the rum flagon and took a swig for courage.

"Pah!" He spat out salty seawater. "Ouch! Ouch!" Two tiny crabs pinched his nose tight.

"'Elp! 'Elp! Getemoff!" He skidded madly round and round on the slippery deck.

"Waaaaaaaaaaaaaah!" He shot past Spirulina, slid down the plank and fell headfirst into the sea.

Spirulina and Jennifer cheered as Shipmate Shifty spluttered about in the water...

...Bony Boson swung upside down in the parrot cage...

...and Captain Curly waved his cutlass uselessly.

"Hooray!
We're saved!"
cried Coralie
and Shelle
in delight.

Spirulina leaped on to the SS *Spirulina* and
Jennifer gave her a push. The little boat
went skidding down the oily deck and
splashed into the sea – headed straight
for home.

With Jennifer on her shoulder, Spirulina scrambled on to Mermaid Rock. Coralie and Shelle clapped and cheered.

They all watched as the great pirate galleon sailed off into the ocean, with Shipmate Shifty swimming after it.

"You saved us, Spirulina," cried Coralie.

"You really are a brave adventurer!" said Shelle.

"It was Jennifer too," Spirulina insisted.

Jennifer shook her feathers in delight.

"Can I have a ride in your boat, Spirulina?" asked Coralie shyly.

"Can I wear your pirate headscarf?" asked Shelle.

"Of course," Spirulina replied, smiling.

They played pirates all afternoon in the sunshine. Coralie and Shelle got great big tangly knots in their hair. But they were having such fun that they didn't care one bit.